Mr Frost

Bu

First published in 2010
by Wayland

Text copyright © Andy Blackford
Illustration copyright © Richard Watson

Wayland
338 Euston Road
London NW1 3BH

Wayland Australia
Level 17/207 Kent Street
Sydney, NSW 2000

Series Editor: Louise John
Cover design: Paul Cherrill
Design: D.R.ink
Consultant: Shirley Bickler

A CIP catalogue record for this book is available from the British Library.

ISBN 9780750262170

Printed in China

Wayland is a division of Hachette Children's Books,
an Hachette UK Company

www.hachette.co.uk

Mr Frost

Written by Andy Blackford
Illustrated by Richard Watson

WAYLAND

When Ruby woke up, her room was very bright. She looked out of her window.

"Look, Merlin, it's snowing!"
she said.

There was so much snow
that Ruby's school was shut.

School Shut

"Hurray!" shouted Ruby.
"Woof!" barked Merlin.

At home, Ruby and Merlin ran into the garden to play.

"Let's build a snowman, Merlin!" said Ruby.

First they made a snowball
for the body.

Then they made a snowball
for the head.

They called the snowman,
Mr Frost.

"We need a hat for Mr Frost!" said Ruby to Merlin.

Merlin got Ruby's pink
bike helmet.

"Go and fetch a carrot for his nose!" said Ruby.

Merlin got a big
green cucumber.

"Now go and fetch some gloves for his hands," said Ruby.

Merlin got Dad's yellow
garden gloves.

"You're a very funny snowman,
Mr Frost," said Ruby.

"Come on, Merlin," said Ruby. "It's time for lunch and Mum has a big bone for you."

Ruby and Merlin went back
to the house.

Just then, a snowball hit
Ruby on the back.

"Grrrr," said Merlin.

"That's funny!" said Ruby.
"No one is there."

But someone **was** there.

"Now I see you, Mr Frost,"
laughed Ruby. "I'll get
you later!"

START READING is a series of highly enjoyable books for beginner readers. **The books have been carefully graded to match the Book Bands widely used in schools.** This enables readers to be sure they choose books that match their own reading ability.

Look out for the Band colour on the book in our Start Reading logo.

The Bands are:

Pink Band 1A & 1B

Red Band 2

Yellow Band 3

Blue Band 4

Green Band 5

Orange Band 6

Turquoise Band 7

Purple Band 8

Gold Band 9

START READING books can be read independently or shared with an adult. They promote the enjoyment of reading through satisfying stories supported by fun illustrations.

Andy Blackford used to play guitar in a rock band. Besides books, he writes about running and scuba diving. He has run across the Sahara Desert and dived with tiger sharks. He lives in the country with his wife and daughter, a friendly collie dog and a grumpy cat.

Richard Watson was born in 1980 and from as soon as he was able to read and write, he always had his nose in a book and a pen in his hand. After school, Richard went on to study illustration in Lincoln and graduated in 2003. He has worked as an illustrator ever since.